Lorraine Aseltine
pictures by Virginia Wright-Frierson

First Grade Can Wait

Albert Whitman & Company
Niles, Illinois

Library of Congress Cataloging-in-Publication Data

Aseltine, Lorraine.
    First grade can wait/Lorraine Aseltine: illustrated by Virginia
Wright-Frierson.
    p. cm.
    Summary: Luke does not feel ready to move on from kinder-
garten to the first grade, and he is relieved when his parents and
teacher decide he can stay in kindergarten for another year.
    ISBN 0-8075-2451-4 (lib.bdg.)
    [1. Kindergarten—Fiction. 2. Schools—Fiction.] I. Wright-
Frierson, Virginia, ill. II. Title.
PZ7.A788Fi 1988   87-26457
[E]—dc19

Luke will be six years old in August.
He goes to kindergarten.
He knows most of his letters and his
numbers from one to twenty.
He knows his shapes very well, too.
He's so good at working puzzles that
sometimes he helps his little sister, Jill.
Luke is a smart boy, but he's not going to
first grade in the fall.
Why not?
He's just not ready yet.

Luke likes lots of things about kindergarten.
He likes singing with the other children.

He likes playing with his friend, Andy.

Most of all, Luke likes art.
He's very good at painting, and sometimes
Miss Armstrong hangs up his pictures.
That makes him feel proud!
Luke likes Miss Armstrong a lot, too.

But there are some things about kindergarten
that are hard for Luke.
He has trouble paying attention when
Miss Armstrong reads stories to the children.
He looks out the window and tries to see
an airplane in the sky.

When Miss Armstrong asks Luke a question,
he is surprised.
He's been thinking about airplanes.
All the children look at him and wait.
He doesn't know what to say.
Miss Armstrong tells Luke to pay attention.
She tells him to pay attention every day,
it seems to Luke.

There are many nice children in Luke's class,
but he's shy and doesn't talk to them much.
He just plays with Andy.
If Andy's not at school, Luke watches
the other children, or he goes off to play
by himself.
Sometimes he brings his yellow truck from
home, but if Andy isn't there, he puts it
back in his schoolbag.
Miss Armstrong asks if he would like to share
his truck with the other boys, but Luke
doesn't want to.

When it's Show and Tell time,
most of the children talk about their birthday
parties or their brothers and sisters.
They show their favorite toys and books.
When Luke tries to talk to the class, the
words don't come out right.
Once he started to cry, and Miss Armstrong
said he could sit down.
Now when it's Luke's turn, he gets a
stomachache.
Last week he wanted to tell how Dad
let him use the camera to take pictures
of the polar bears at the zoo.
Polar bears are his favorite animal.
Luke showed the pictures, but he didn't say
much, even though Miss Armstrong asked
questions to help him.

After spring vacation Miss Armstrong takes
the class for a visit to the first-grade room.
Mrs. Brown, the first-grade teacher, shows
the children some books.
She says everyone will learn how to read them
in first grade.
She talks about work papers first-graders
must take home to show Mom and Dad.

Luke is worried.
He can't remember all the sounds
the letters make.
How will he ever learn to read?
And he doesn't always remember the directions
for the work papers in kindergarten.
How will he ever do papers in first grade?
After supper, Luke tells Dad about the visit
to the first-grade room.
Luke says he didn't like it very much.

The next day, when the class goes out to play,
Luke gets his shoes and pants all wet.
Miss Armstrong looks serious.
She wants to know what happened.
Luke remembers that she told the children to
stay out of puddles.
He sees everyone looking at him.
He wants to tell Miss Armstrong that Nicholas
accidentally pushed him into a deep puddle,
but he can't say anything!
Luke just stands there with his head down.
He feels the water go *squish* inside his shoes.

As soon as Luke gets home from school,
he gives Mom a note from Miss Armstrong.
He tells Mom that Nicholas accidentally
pushed him into the puddle.
"Why didn't you tell Miss Armstrong?"
Mom asks Luke.
Luke shakes his head. "I don't know," he says.
Mom hugs him and tells him not to worry.
She says she will talk to Miss Armstrong
and explain everything.

In the morning, it's Mom's turn to drive the children to school.
She doesn't go home right away.
She talks to Miss Armstrong.
Luke wonders what they are saying.
He thinks they are talking about him.
He feels better when he sees Mom smiling.

After supper Mom, Dad, Luke, and Jill play
toss and catch in the backyard.
Luke knows how to throw the ball right to Jill,
and he feels good about that.
But he can't catch it very often when Dad
throws it to him.
This makes him unhappy.
Jill can't catch the ball very well, either,
but she's only three.
When Luke keeps missing, he gets mad.
He doesn't want to play anymore.
He runs into the house.

Mom and Dad come in and sit on Luke's bed.
Dad says he's noticed that Luke is worried
about how well he can play ball and about a lot
of other things, too.
Mom wonders if Luke is worrying about
going to first grade.

All of a sudden Luke starts to talk and cry
at the same time.
He says he is afraid to go to first grade.
He doesn't think he can learn how to read.
He doesn't want a new teacher.
He likes Miss Armstrong!
He feels awful because he can't play ball
very well.

Mom and Dad hug Luke hard.

Dad says that Luke doesn't have to worry.
Children don't have to hurry to grow up.
Luke has lots of time to learn to read and
catch a ball.
Dad measures Luke against the wall to show
him how much he's grown in just a few months.
He reminds Luke that last year he didn't even
know his numbers up to twenty—and now
he does!
Mom says maybe Luke is a little too young
for first grade.
Some of the other children are already six,
but Luke won't be six until August.
Miss Armstrong says he can stay in
kindergarten another year.
Children often do this.
Miss Armstrong is sure that in a year Luke
will really want to go to first grade.

Luke feels a little better.
He thinks that maybe he *is* too young for
first grade.
When Mom and Dad tuck him into bed, he tells
them he would like to stay in Miss Armstrong's
room for just one more year.

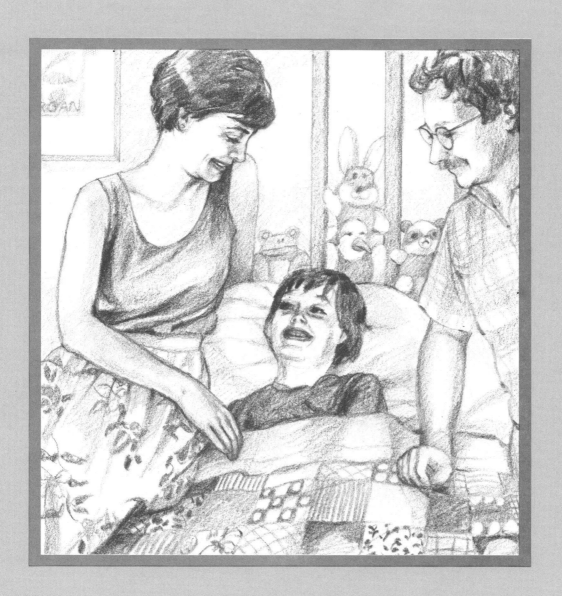

Today Luke feels good about school.
When Miss Armstrong asks him a question
about the story she's reading, he can tell her
the answer right away.
She doesn't have to tell him to pay attention.
Miss Armstrong smiles at Luke, and he
smiles back.

Luke is glad he's not going to first grade
next year.
He's just getting used to kindergarten.

Lorraine Aseltine has worked extensively with young children. Perhaps the most important result of her time spent with preschool hearing-impaired children was *I'm Deaf and It's Okay*, written in collaboration with two colleagues. As a liaison between kindergarten and preschool teachers, she gained special insight into the importance of giving children enough time to grow emotionally and socially. At present she is helping children improve their basic reading skills.

Lorraine lives in Lombard, Illinois, with her husband, Jim. They enjoy their two sons, twin daughters, and eight grandchildren, as well as walking, bird watching, and reading.

Virginia Wright-Frierson lives in Wilmington, North Carolina, a few minutes from the beach, with her math-professor husband, three-year-old daughter, and nine-year-old son. They were all used as models in this book.

She earned a BFA degree in painting at the University of North Carolina at Greensboro and has studied at the Art Students League in New York, the University of Arizona, and a University of Georgia Studies Abroad program in Cortona, Italy.

Ms. Wright-Frierson has exhibited her watercolors and oils in museums and galleries since 1970 and often gives workshops in life drawing, landscape painting, and still life. She has illustrated two other books for children.